THE REBEL

NATHAN JOHNSON

BLUEPRINT PRESS
INTERNATIONALE

ISBN
978-1-961117-60-0 (Paperback)
978-1-961117-61-7 (eBook)
978-1-961117-59-4 (Hardcover)

TABLE OF CONTENTS

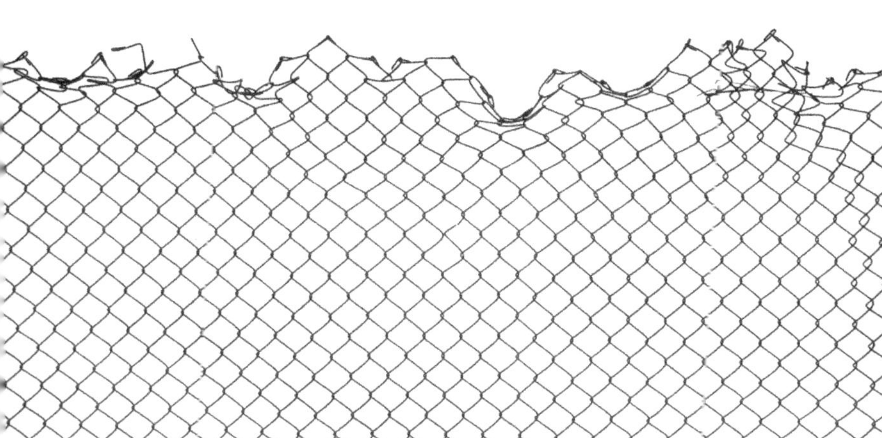

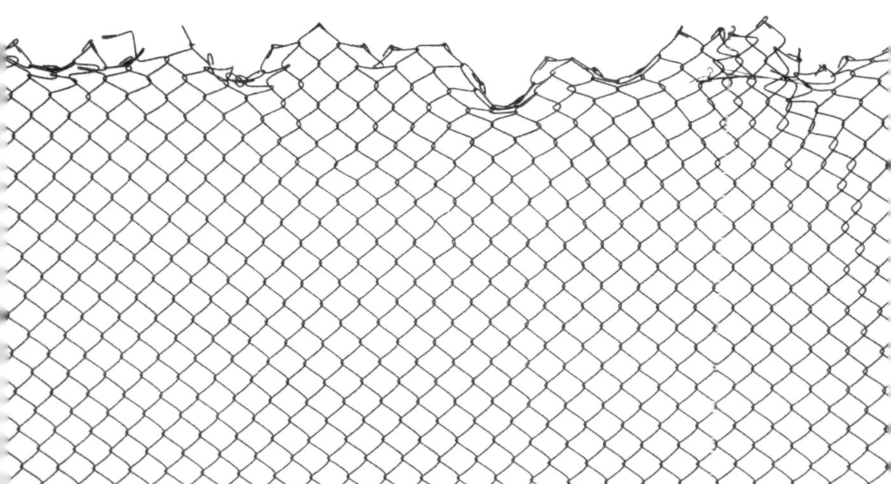

PART ONE

The Mistakes of a Parent: The Life of John Cooper from August 1957 to December 1961

August 1957

Hello, most of you don't know me. Don't worry, you will after I explain myself. I'm John Cooper. I'm now a successful businessman, but I was a rebel. Not that I caused trouble, but I rebelled against my father's actions. It started the day I was born, March 27, 1949, in Birmingham, Alabama. I believe God put here to work toward good values in my family and my home. My older brother, James, was born May 14, 1947, younger brother, Joe, was born Jun. 24, 1959. I felt James and Joe were spoiled and my dad blamed me for everything. In Summer1957, James/I was on our way to the pond. He never liked me tagging along:

Me: "Hey James, where are you going?"

James: "Away from you."

Me: "Why would you want to get away from me?"

James: "Because you're an idiot."

Me: "I haven't done anything to deserve that! I asked a simple question!"

James: "Daddy!"

Daddy: "What's going on here? I'm watching TV and don't have time for this!"

James: "John is trying to pick a fight and I want to hit him!"

Daddy: "John, go to your room! Don't come out until I tell you!"

Me: Don't you want to hear what happened?"

Daddy: "NO! Go to your room, NOW!"

Every time James/I had a discussion, I was sent to my room. No worries, I had mama on my side. She always bailed me out:

Mama: "Hello, where's John? He's normally running to me when I get home. What have you done now?"

Daddy: "He's in his room. He was arguing with James again!'"

Mama: "Lord have mercy, why does John always have to suffer? We both know James usually starts. He probably asked 'What do you need' or 'where are you going?'

Daddy: "I don't care! You're the one who wanted him, not me!"

Mama: "He's coming out and playing, like a normal eight year old. Your parenting skills are the worst and you're a terrible father!"

Daddy: "His punishment will be much worse next time. He needs to wake up to reality, like I did!"

I heard the argument and loved every minute of it. She told it like it was and I agreed! He WAS a lousy father and uncaring person. I always trusted mama in that regard. When he sent me to my room I waited for her to tell me to come out. Daddy was mean and I knew we needed to leave him. A perfect example of this came to light on the school playground. My best friend Jimmy was in trouble. Bruce Jones tried to make him eat dirt.

Brewer Elementary School- January 1958

"Bruce: "What's the matter, Jimmy? Afraid to eat dirt? Oh come on, I'll give you my lunch for a week!"

Jimmy was very shy and didn't like to fight. Bruce was the school bully and not well liked. He rubbed his face in the dirt and that was it!

Me: "Hey fool, leave him alone or you'll be in the dirt! You know he's my best friend! Leave him be!" Bruce: "Who do you think you are, punk?"

Me: "Never mind. Don't start nothing and there won't be nothing!"

Bruce: "I'm not scared of you, punk! Get out of here NOW!"

Me: "Don't say I didn't warn you!"

Bruce: "Oh yeah? Well, take this!"

When Bruce swung, I blocked his punch and knocked him to the dirt, pinning him to the ground:

Me: "Now, are you going to leave Jimmy alone?! HUH? (Holding him harder and harder, not allowing him to move until he agreed).*

Thirty minutes later, I was called to Principal Jack Baines' office. I still don't how he knew because there were no teachers present during the altercation. Regardless, I was in serious trouble:

Baines: "I understand you got into a fight. What happened and why?"

Me: "Well sir, Bruce Jones was bothering my friend Jimmy and I took up for him. I tried to get him to stop, but he wouldn't.

Baines: "Why didn't you talk to you teacher, instead of confronting him?"

Me: "I couldn't find her. After I asked him to stop, he tried to hit me and I defended myself."

Baines: "That wouldn't have happened if you'd looked for your teacher. I appreciate you trying to help, but you can't take matters into your own hands, just like a citizen can't take matters into his/her own hands when a crime has been committed. Do you understand? I'm afraid I have to paddle you."

Me: "I'm sorry and I know I was wrong, but shouldn't Bruce be paddled too?"

Baines: "Bend over."

That was my luck. I knew I should've gone to my teacher, but protecting Jimmy was my first instinct. It was no big deal. Bruce/I were friends after that. I had bigger problems when I got home. I didn't tell my parents because I knew I'd get paddled. I didn't have to tell them, James did!"

Daddy: "Is there something you need to tell me?

Me: "No, not that I remember."

Daddy: "You got paddled today, didn't you? (Shouting) WELL, DIDN'T YOU?!"

Me: "*Yeah.*"

James: "HA! HA! I told on you!"

Me: "WHAT?! You said you wouldn't blab! I didn't when you got paddled last week for smoking in the restroom!"

Daddy: "No matter, you're still getting paddled! I don't care what the excuse!"

I grabbed my ankles, expecting the worst. Then, much to my surprise, mama made him stop!

Mama: "Oh, no you don't, you're NOT spanking John, especially if James didn't get in trouble last week! I'm so tired of this!"

Daddy: "Stay out of this, woman! That's the trouble, you don't know when to keep your mouth shut!"

Mama: (Screaming): "THAT DOES IT! I'm disciplining our children from now on! I'll let you spank John this time ONLY, but if you do, I'll spank James. Come on! Make it good, this will be the last time!"

That said, daddy threw the paddle on the floor.

Mama was great! Daddy never tried to discipline, at least while she was around. However, mama wasn't always there and daddy still got his way. I tried to live as "normal" a life as possible. Mama struggled to make it as normal as possible too. To this day, she still sends money even though I don't need it. Daddy and I weren't close and there was no love between us. I didn't go to his funeral when he died in 1984, at age 61. However, despite their troubles, they had another child.

June 1959

Everything was better with mom in control, especially with a new addition to the family. On Jun. 24, 1959, my brother Joe was born. Daddy was nice for a change. He promised me things would be different. Could it be true?

Daddy: "That's my boy. Isn't he cute?"

Me: "Uh, *Yeah.*"

Daddy: "Come on, John, say hello to your new brother. Do you want to hold him?"

Me: "Can I really?"

Daddy: "Of course! Why do you ask? I know we've had our disagreements, but I'd like to start over!"

Me: "Great! I'd love to do more with you!"

Daddy: "Well, then it's settled."

Me: "Thank you very much!"

I felt so stupid for believing this bull! The niceness lasted for about a month. Then it was back to the same old stuff, except much worse! Mama started giving the baby more attention, neglecting me and James, meaning daddy was more out of control than ever! His promise meant nothing and I'd had it! He'd spank before I went to school and when I got home in case I got in trouble there. I understood that mama had to take care of the baby, but I was becoming one of those rebels I told you about earlier.

January 1960- The "Rebel" Begins to Surface

Daddy: "Don't you dare walk out on me! It'll only be worse if you don't take your medicine!"

Me: "I'm not coming back! I've been taking medicine for almost 11 years and I won't take anymore!"

Mama: "Please stay! I promise it'll be better! Daddy didn't mean what he said! Please Stay!"

Me: "I'm not coming back, not until you get rid of daddy!"

I stayed with Butch Jones for five days. I only came back because mama talked me into it. Besides I had to do something because I was in trouble in school. Mama never neglected me again, but daddy was still the problem. Butch was a terrible influence, making me do things I can't mention in this story. It all involved drugs, stealing and smoking. He was the ringleader of our gang in the early '60s. He was fourteen and I was eleven. The more I was around him the more trouble I was in. In three months, I had a brief addiction to morphine.

I rarely came home to avoid daddy. The more I stayed away, the better. One cold night, Butch/I egged a car and were arrested:

Me: I'm bored! We must find something to do! I'm going crazy!"

Butch: "Oh, you are huh?"

Me: "Yeah, I sure am."

Butch: "I know what you mean! Hey! I have a great idea! I have a three cartons of eggs in the fridge! Have you ever gone egging?"

Me: "No."

Butch: "Well you're about to! Let's hit the dealership!"

Me: "Cool, let's do it!"

For thirty minutes, we were having a blast. After the first carton, I felt guilty. I knew we shouldn't have been there, but I couldn't talk Butch out of it. Then, a dreaded thing happened:

Me: "Man, egging is a blast!"

Butch: "Get down!"

Me: "Why?"

Butch: "The fuzz is here!"

Me: "The fuzz??"

Butch: "The police, dummy!"

It was too late! We were at the station faster than we could blink. Furthermore I was fined $200. This wasn't Butch's first offense and he was sentenced to eight months in juvenile. The parents posted bail and I was grounded for six months. I was glad in many ways because I thought it might give me a chance at a normal childhood. However, that wasn't the case.

February 1960-February 1961. Home Again

I had been home a year and daddy seemed to be much better. It seemed he had changed. My best friend, Jimmy, came over every day and we played like normal children. Daddy took us to baseball and football games and we all sat at the dinner table like a traditional family. The first six months was a little rough being grounded, but at least we were a normal family.

Daddy: "John, I have a confession."

Me: "What is it?"

Daddy: "I haven't treated you fairly. I've let you down."

Me: "I'm glad you realize. It's only taken eleven years."

Daddy: "I've been stressed out at work. I'll be the father you never had."

Me: "I agree, if you keep your end of the deal."

Daddy: "I'll try, but I can't promise anything."

Me: "That's all I ask."

Mama wasn't convinced. He promised her the same thing and she no longer believed it. She wanted to leave. However, she honored my plea and gave him another chance, reassuring me, James and Joe that if he went back to his old ways, we'd leave.

Mama was right and come December, mama made him leave. I started hanging with Butch again and we were getting into trouble. I couldn't seem to find a since of belonging any other way. All Butch/I did was terrorize the neighborhood.

We knew kids who were pretty bad, but even they didn't seem bad anymore. In fact, we formed a gang and they were incorporated into it. I was still at home, but daddy's empty promise was had finally driven me to this.

End of Part I

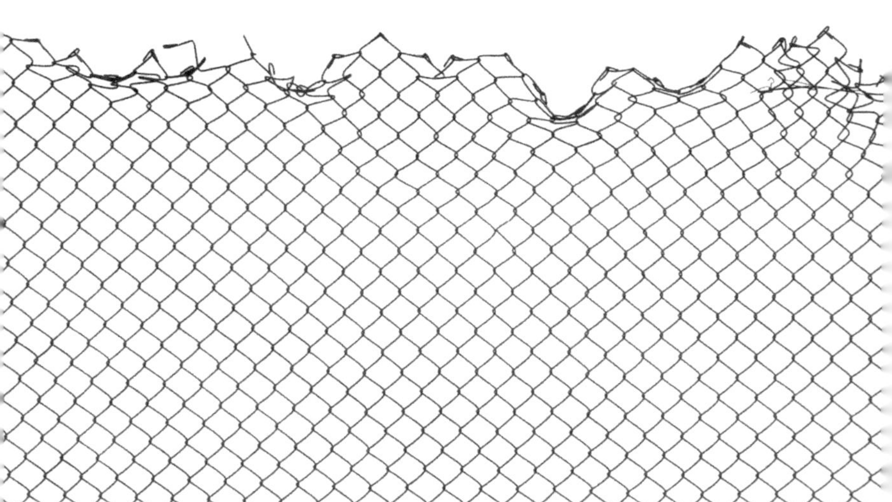

PART TWO

The Gang for Troubled Children:
The Life of John Cooper from
January 1962 to January 1963.

January 1962- The Beginning of the Gang

Save the date- Jan. 3, 1962, 2pm. The inaugural meeting of the Bad Boys Gang (BBG). It included boys, like myself, who had terrible childhoods and felt like we had to take it out on others. They included myself, Butch Jones, Mike Johns, and Ritchie June. Butch was 15, Mike was 13, Richie was 12, was almost 13. Butch was the oldest, so he led us. We carried rebel flags wore rebel shirts and had racial fights. I learned how to fight and learn how to use a knife. Our slogan was "We don't take nothing from nobody." That sounds very simple, but people who join gangs are not very intelligent, at least at our ages. Within three months, we were the most feared boys in town.

Mama didn't know what to do. She, James, and Joe were worried. They knew trouble wasn't far away for me. In April, talked to me about dropping out, but my mind was made up. However, it reassured me she cared. I wish she had succeeded because in May, I got in trouble and was arrested again. Daddy was upset, only because I got caught!

The Arrest

"All right, boys, let's go back to the station. I finally caught you! Congratulations! You're part of the system now, or at least you will be!"

I'll never forget those very discouraging words, but Officer Blanchard was right. It was where I was headed. We were arrested for fighting with The Serpents, a rebel gang, at school. After months of fighting and rioting, our luck finally ran out.

When mama and daddy came to bail me out, she was relieved and daddy was furious. This added insult to injury because all that happened was daddy/I got in to get into it again. As expected, daddy/I got into another huge fight. However, I chose to come home because of mama:

Daddy: "You should be whipped for joining that gang! WHY DID YOU GET CAUGHT?! You sorry excuse for a son! Why do I even bother with you?!"

Me: "You're a sorry excuse for a father! You're the reason why I joined A GANG in the first place! Don't EVER talk down to like that again!"

Daddy (Shaking his fist): "Don't you EVER talk to me like that again, or I'll KILL you!"

After he said that I went into the kitchen and grabbed a steak knife went over to daddy.

Me: "You poor excuse for a father! You slime! You bastard! You son of a buck, now here, KILL ME, I DARE YOU!"

I even put the knife in his hand!

Mama: "I completely agree with Johnny. I can't let you be around the boys anymore. I want you to leave and if you EVER come back, I WILL call the police! Our son is in a gang and he has a record. That's all the reason I need.

At that moment, daddy gave mama the cold shoulder, walked out of the house and got into the car.

A few days later daddy "disowned" me. Imagine that! The summer of '62 was nice. I was very glad to be home, despite being financially strapped. It gave me a chance to bond with

James and Joe. Meanwhile, daddy lost his job. He took this as an opportunity to seek help.

In September, it came to an abrupt end. Mama/Daddy agreed among themselves that he should get visitation rights. I argued with her over it and before I knew it, I rejoined the BBG. I knew it wasn't the answer, but anything was better than seeing daddy!

Back to the Gang- Sept. 1962

By the time school started, mama was worried sick again and daddy was at The Haven. The gang was more notorious than ever- "School kids by day, gang members by night. In November, I mama sent a letter concerning daddy. He had "mood disorders" and agreed on medication. She wanted me home for the holidays, but I wrote her back and told her I wanted to spend them with the gang. I also said I was still making A's and B's, so she hopefully took comfort in that

In Feb. 1963, daddy was released from the Haven. He wrote and asked me to come see him, but I knew it was a bad idea. I was back in Juvenile by September 1963. I wasn't in trouble, but the gang folded and Officer Blanchard knew I couldn't take care of myself at 14.After a few days there, I talked to mama and we agreed it was best to come home and I did. I kept a copy of daddy's letter dated March 21, 1963:

Dear John,

I'm writing because I'm out of Psychiatric Treatment. I'm taking three different medications for my mood disorders. I'd apologize for the argument we had last

May. I hope you'll visit me soon. I really have missed you. I'll make it up to you. Looking forward seeing you."

Love,
Daddy

**This letter was used as evidence in daddy's trial. He was convicted and sent to prison on Jun. 16, 1967.*

The letter hung daddy many times. As you'd expect, he didn't mean it. He only wanted to see me so he could enroll me in Mobile Detention Center. In Oct. 1963, I went to see him. It was a HUGE mistake! I gave him the benefit of the doubt. He also lied about taking his medicine. It was only a ploy to get me out of the way. He already had me enrolled for Jan. 15, 1964. My start date was Jan. 15, 1964. Mama tried to stop him, but it was too late. I <u>was</u> going and that was that!

January 1964. Mobile Alabama Detention Center

Me: "Why don't you go away and leave us alone? I wish you wouldn't make me go there!"

Daddy: "DON'T GIVE ME THAT! You know why you're going! You're no good and it's where you belong! END OF DISCUSSION!"

Me: "I'm pleading with you! Don't make me go!"

Daddy: "OH, so now you want to plead! I LOVE IT! You sure were defiant back in May! NOW you're pleading! HA! HA! Anyway, you mad your bed, now you must lie in it!"

Me: "Yeah, and whose fault is that? If you'd been a father, I wouldn't be here! Thanks to you, I'm stuck!"

Daddy: "Oh well, you should've never been born! Now you'll be out of my way."

Me: "Well, the feeling is mutual! YOU MAKE ME SICK! I just want you to know that!"

Daddy: "You make me sick too! I wish you had never been born!"

Then he walked away.

Daddy arranged for me to stay for two years. The day he dropped me off is dubbed as "The first day of hell." Oh well, it is what it is. Two years isn't a lifetime. I'd survive and daddy would pay.

End of Part II

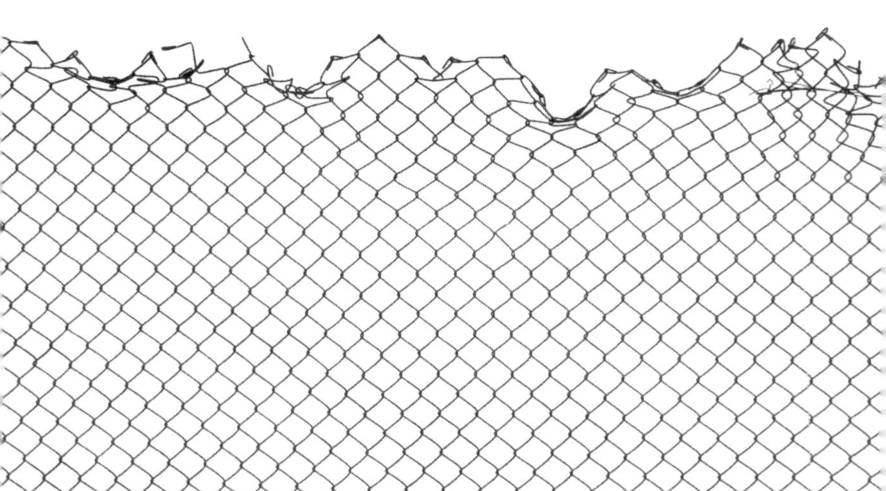

PART THREE

Juvenile Detention: They Either Get
Better or Worse: The Life of John Cooper
from January 1963 to June 1966

January 15, 1964- The Worst Day of My Life

Here I sat, asking myself "Why me?" Why must I be punished? I guess because daddy's crazy and I'm a victim. All I need is love and understanding? Is that too much to ask? I only wish mama could do more. Oh well, no one could've seen this coming. Oh well, all I can do is make the best of it.

Now for the fun! I must eat lunch with my new peers. Too bad it's mandatory! It's already been the worst day of my life, so why not make it worse? That way, I can measure this moment as the nadir in my life! After meeting my new peers, I learned most of them were three times as bad. For example, Mick Johnston. He and I became good friends. This wasn't good because he could've easily corrupted me. Honestly, I learned how to get into trouble with the BBG, but I'm very glad to say I never went along with them. I had a conscience and never did what they told me. I also discovered Mick had some of the same problems as me, so I felt like I was in the same boat with him.

Mick: "Hi, I'm Mick. What's your name? I haven't seen you before. First day?"

Me: "I'm John Cooper. Yes, first day."

Mick: "I thought so.

Me: "How do you know?"

Mick: "You look so innocent.

Me: "I don't belong here and I'm not going to be negatively influenced. I'm not that innocent. I was in a gang and there isn't anything I haven't seen. My only plan is to follow the rules and get out of here."

Mick: "Same here. I'm tired of doing wrong and bullying people around. I'm here to change my life too. What are you in for?"

Me: "My daddy enrolled me because he wants me out of his way. That's why I was in a gang because my father mistreated me and I needed a way out, so when he wrote me and told me things were going to be different, I went back and he trapped me and threw me in here."

Mick: "Man, that's rough. It sounds like my dad. Only, I had no intention of changing."

Me: "Why are you here?"

Mick: "Armed Robbery."

Me: "Yes, my gang members were into that. It's why I decided to come home."

Mick: "I have to stay three more years until I'm eighteen."

Me: "Sorry to hear that."

Mick: "That's okay. I'm good with it. I intend to get on with my life after this."

Me: "Yeah, I'll be fifteen next month."

Mick: "You'll make it. I have faith."

And I thought I was the only one with problems. If it wasn't for daddy, I wouldn't be in this rat hole. The floors were dirty, the rooms were cold and it always smelled. It was hell, only it wasn't hot!

Mick and I were great friends. In fact, we went to college together. We got in trouble for normal teenage things, but that was about it. It wasn't too bad. One month down, twenty eight to go. Hopefully they'll go by as quickly as this one.

My family came to visit in April. James/Joe even came, and unfortunately, so did daddy! I wish he'd have stayed home and laid an egg, but that didn't happen! James mentioned that daddy was hitting Joe with a razor strap every time he asked why he was being punished. He did the same thing to James. The worst was what he did to mama. I was livid! James moved in to protect her. I hoped daddy would lose visitation rights with Joe.

Mama: "Hi son!"

Me: "Oh mama, I missed you. How are things at home?"

Mama: "Not good. Daddy doesn't understand the divorce terms."

Me: "No surprise there!"

Mama: "That's the other reason I came. Now, please listen to me. It's important."

Me: "Sure."

Mama: "I have a restraining order against daddy."

Me: "Ok."

Mama: "That's not all. He's here."

Me: "I don't want to see him!"

Mama: "Hold on. Let me finish."

Me: "Sorry, go ahead."

Mama: "I need to tell you something. Last month, he broke into the house, threw me on the bed hit me! That's the reason for the restraining order."

Me: (Yelling): "That's horrible! I'M GOING TO KILL HIM!"

Mama; "Honey, I've said the same thing many times, but I can't bring myself to do it and neither can you. I've already warned him. If he does it again, I'll shoot him! I'll let you talk to James/Joe. Now, Daddy will be in to see you in a minute and you can say whatever you want. I know you're very angry and you have the right to tell him how you feel. Be very careful of what you say. He has the judge in his favor."

Me: "I know about him bribing the judge, but I'm not walking on eggshells either."

Mama: "You don't have to, just a warning."

Me: "Don't worry. I'll handle it. You go and I'll see you next month."

Mama: "Okay. I love you."

Me: "Love you too."

A few minutes later, daddy came in. He was unaware I knew about the restraining order. I already had permission from mama, James and even Joe. He knew EXACTLY how upset I was. He could see it!

Me: "How dare you show your face here!?"

Daddy: "Don't talk to me like that, boy!"

Me: "You're right! I shouldn't talk to you like that! I was too nice! You're a horrible person, I want you to know that! You deserve anything bad that happens! I hope you ROT!"

Daddy: "I hope you do too! HOW'S THAT!?"

Me: "NO DADDY! THAT'S YOU'RE JOB! You are a crazy fool and you have no right to be in my life! I will get out of here! Yes, I'm a REBEL, but I have a cause and that's to see you in prison to ROT!"

Daddy: "Very well, but I have the power! Don't push me!"

After that, he walked out.

January 1965

Jan. 15 was my first anniversary at Mobile Detention. It was also the day the daddy's restraining order began. He couldn't come within 1000 feet of my family until September 30. I was very proud to give my consent to mama to allow it to happen. After that, who knew how it would work out?

After the argument with daddy, James/I knew I had to get out of here. It's hard to believe James dealt with him that long, seeing as I'd avoided home since 1960. I knew James couldn't much, but all he could do was try. However, Daddy had entirely too much control, which meant I was likely here until June 1966, per the agreement. I also discovered that shortly before mama filed the restraining order, daddy broke into the house again, hit her, knocking her through the front door. She said she tried to shoot him, but he was already gone before she got the gun.

Mama: "John, I have a restraining order against daddy."

Me: "Why?"

Mama: "Because I want to keep our family safe. Besides, James/Joe are becoming more like him every day. But that's not why I'm here. I'm trying to get you out. James told me he wanted to help, but there isn't much he can do. However, the judge heard his case and he wants to help. He's aware daddy bribed him, but he claims he only accepted because he knows how daddy is and wants to help put him away. Not sure I believe him, but that's beside the point. Having said that, don't get your hopes up. Just pray about it, okay?

Me: "Will do, keep me posted."

That was encouraging! I still hate it here, but it gave me hope! Daddy's restraining order was up in September, and I need to go to court with the family to persuade the judge for an extension. Mama's visit was quickly soured when it was daddy turn to visit later that day. I was, however, optimistic.

Daddy (Laughing): "I'm telling you, boy, a restraining order doesn't mean you won't be here until June of next year. I knew you'd be disappointed if I didn't tell you! I know how much you LOVE it here!"

Me: "And I said I didn't EVER want to see you again! So what are you doing here?! You're not my daddy! I disowned you, remember? Sure, you're my birth father, but you're not a father!"

Daddy (Finger pointed at my face): "I'd watch it, if I were you? I CAN and WILL use that against you!"

Me: "GO AHEAD! I many much more ammunition and I WILL use it! Good day, daddy!"

Daddy: "Don't push it."

Daddy's visit proved costly and his restraining order was extended, as he was in violation of the order! Mama wanted us to testify in an attempt to also get him on child abuse charges. The hearing also determined that I may get out early, but whatever happened, it was a relief knowing daddy was convicted of child abuse and forever banned from the family, not to mention an extension of the restraining order until May 1966!

September 1965

The only drawback was that daddy bribed the judge $1500 to keep me in Mobile Detention until June 1966. However, we made a deal with Judge Harper that if daddy tried to bribe him, he'd accept it and put him on report. As expected, *he took the bait and all it required was another nine months in Mobile Detention!*

September 30, 1965- More Trouble for Daddy

Mobile, Alabama Detention Center

Mick: "Don't look now, but your daddy is on his way! I see him through the window!"

Me: "What?! It IS him. Why in the Sam Hill is he here?!"

Mick: "You know him, he's crazier than me!"

Me: "I know that's right! Don't worry about me! I'll handle it!"

Mick: "I know you will."

At the front desk, daddy looked seriously angry. He was here and there was nothing anyone could do to stop him!

Secretary: "Mr. Cooper, you can't be here! Judge's orders, I must ask you to leave!"

Daddy: "I came to see my son and I'm not leaving until I do! Now, am I going to see him, or am I going to kill you, him and everyone here?"

Secretary: "I'll call John!"

I'd already told the secretary that daddy was here and after she said she'd call me down, she was really calling the police.

Me: "Daddy, you must leave now."

Daddy: "Can't I see my own son?"

Me: "NO! GET LOST!"

Daddy: "Don't speak to me like that again BOY, or I'll KILL you!"

Me: "The have been notified and they're on their way! You have a chance to leave now. I suggest you go!"

Daddy: "You're lying. You're too chicken to call them!"

Me: "Trust me, they've been notified! They'll be here in ten minutes."

Ten minutes later, they were there and I could tell Officer Johnson wasn't happy. I was even afraid for daddy!

Officer Johnson: "You again?! I'm very tired of dealing with you! YOU ARE UNDER ARREST!"

Daddy: "YOU CAN'T DO THAT! JOHN, bail me out! If you don't, I'll KILL YOU!"

Me: "I didn't want this either, but I warned you!"

Daddy: "Watch this!"

Daddy punched Officer Johnson and his backup knocked him out with a club, handcuffed him and had him in the car within ten seconds!

Two Weeks Later

As rain fell over the hard ground this morning after 46 days without rain, I had showered and was almost ready to go to breakfast. I'd be a free man in seven months. After my smoke break at 9, I went downstairs to eat. It was nothing out of the ordinary, so why am I talking about it? Because, it was a special day. Mama, James and Joe were coming at 11. They also had good news; another attempt releasing me early! I couldn't wait until 11 and when the time came, I rushed to meet them!

Hoping for the Best

Mama: "Do you think John will be released in March?"

Mrs. Poole: "Mrs. Cooper, it's going to be very difficult. The agreed date is Jun. 20. In fact, if Mr. Cooper can arrange for a later date, he likely won't leave until he's eighteen, but you know I'm trying. My hands are tied. Wish the news was better."

Mama: "We just have to pray it doesn't happen. He deserves a normal life."

Mrs. Poole: "I understand. If it were up to me, you could have him now, but there's very little chance of that. I'll talk to the judge again. I'll do my best."

Mama: "I know you will. If my ex-husband has anything to say about it, he'd go to prison after he turns eighteen."

Mrs. Poole: "I wouldn't worry. I promise Mr. Cooper doesn't have that kind of pull. Besides, John is a model student, which is in his favor, but Mr. Cooper is still very much in control for now."

Mama: "Thanks for trying. I guess I'll tell John the news."

Mrs. Poole: "I'll keep you posted."

Mama: "Thanks."

When mama came in, I knew it was bad news. As she explained the situation, all I could do was comfort her. All I could do was think positive.

Me: "Hi Mama, it's nice to see you again. It seems like forever since the last time. At least daddy is in his place for now."

Mama: "That's the problem! They've released him again. Nothing will change until or unless they keep him there. He's already harassing me again."

Me: "Why won't he leave us be?"

Mama: "If I knew that I'd be a rocket scientist! He knows I'll call the police if he comes. I also have my gun. He doesn't seem to be afraid of the police."

Me: "That's why they call me The Rebel."

Mama (Laughing): "I know what you mean, but that's what it takes. Well, you take care. James/Joe will be here soon.

Me: "Okay, take care. Watch out for daddy."

Mama: "I will. Love you."

Me: "Love you too!"

After that, James walks in.

Me: "James, how are you?"

James: "Oh, great. I'm still at home and I have a car!"

Me: "I heard! What kind?"

James: "A 1954 Dodge. Nothing fancy, but it gets me where I'm going."

Me: "Just be careful."

James: "I am. Why are you telling me to be careful?"

Me (Joking): "I'm told you're a crazy driver! You should purchase a burial policy!"

James: "HA! HA! You're ALMOST as funny as that train wreck I saw on TV the other night. Surely, you can do better than that!"

Me: "You're right! It would've been a riot if you were in it when it exploded and your face would've been black like Yosemite Sam's! You know I'm joking! I'm looking forward to spending time with you/Joe."

James: "Same here. We really get along now. Well, my time is up. See you later."

Me: "Ok. Hopefully daddy will go to prison soon!"

James: "Hopefully."

Sadly, that was the best visit James/I had to date. Little Joe didn't say much. He's rather shy and quiet. I think he was either afraid of me was too young to understand. Either way, he was scared. He had a raw deal and didn't know how to behave. He learned to keep quiet, rather than say anything that might've gotten him into trouble. It was difficult enough for me at sixteen, much less for him at six. It was definitely something we'd work out later, when I was out.

In the meantime, daddy was in trouble again. He kept showing up like a bad penny. Any excuse he found to come back, he took. We kept praying he'd leave us for good, but it never seemed to happen. Each time he was much more aggressive than the time before and it ALWAYS had to be on poor mama!

December 12, 1965. Daddy's 2nd Restraining Order Violation

The reason *I remember that day is because I was reading my Bible as I did every Sunday morning. Mama brought it to me last time I saw her. I had finished reading at 9 o'clock when the phone rang. It was her. She told me daddy almost broke in the house with a pistol and shot her. I was really shocked and I handled it with my normal response. I told her once again that I was going to kill him. As always, she calmed me down.*

Daddy was going bowling with his buddies and he wanted inside to get his ball. She told him she'd put in on the porch as soon as she could find it. Daddy wouldn't have it that way. He wanted to come in and get it himself, which was in violation of the restraining order. One could only imagine what happened next.

Daddy: "Woman, you better let me in or I'll kill you!"

Mama (Pointing her pistol at him): "Look, I told you I'd put the damn ball out on the porch as soon as I find it. Apparently, you haven't figured it out yet. It's either going to be my way, or you can live without it. You know I don't want to shoot you but I will. I'm not playing games anymore! You've already ruined John's life and James has to put himself out just to help us make ends meet. I'll be damned if you're going to ruin Joe's life too. Besides, he's been through enough already! Now take that bowling ball and get out of my sight before I pull the trigger!"

Daddy: "I'll be back! I won't be through until I get my children back!"

After that, mama called the police. Daddy was too stupid to realize he almost got killed that night. Mama told me later that if he'd tried to come in the house that night, she would've pulled the trigger and shot him at point blank range, just as she'd threatened. Deep down, I really think daddy knew that, hence why he left. Actually, I'm amazed he lived another 18 years! Meanwhile, the police stopped daddy in the car on the way to the bowling alley, arrested him, and took him to jail. Bowling would certainly have to wait another night.

Daddy: "What the hell is your problem now?!"

Officer Johnson: "I have a complaint from Mrs. Cooper and we have to take you back to jail."

Daddy (Yelling): "That's the second time this year!"

Officer Johnson: "You're right! You can count, good job! When are you going to learn? Apparently you don't realize that we're very serious about this! If you still want to argue, I'll slap you with another violation, take you in, and jack your bail up so high Elvis Presley couldn't afford it, so do you want to argue, or cooperate?"

Realizing he had no choice, he cooperated with Officer Johnson, and served his jail time. By now, daddy's luck was running out. The police were getting very tired of coming after him all the time. It wasn't going to be long now.

One Month Later

Today was special. I've got two years down and five months to go. It'd been a battle and I'd already missed many great things most kids took for granted. However, believe it or not, I really enjoyed the education I received while I was in Mobile. I was very fortunate to have great teachers and to this day, I'm still very good friends with many of them. I was now the equivalent of a junior in high school.

I 'd already decided to go to college and major in business Better yet, I got to enjoy my senior year in high school. My grades transferred from Mobile Alabama Correction Center. Birmingham High School was impressed with my grades at the time I transferred, especially having been in juvenile. I was very eager to learn about a whole new world I hadn't been able to enjoy for two and a half years.

I'd never had a chance to live, but I was still young. I was still on pace to graduate in May 1967.

My family threw me a party at the center. We celebrated the fact that I'd be out in less than six months. Daddy was still causing problems, so it didn't look good for us this year either. For about a month, he'd laid low, but we hadn't heard the last of him. You could bet on that!

February 1966. Daddy Violates Protective Order Again

It turned out I was right, daddy been quiet for too long. In fact, everyone knew he'd strike again, just didn't know when. Then, it finally happened. It goes to show I knew him well. However, there was one twist to this one that struck me as strange. It was not mama he harassed this time, it was James. Looking back, I wasn't too surprised since it was obvious mama would kill him. He went to James because he thought he'd back down to him and let him have his way. In a nutshell, he threatened James by saying he would "Kill him" if he didn't come to live with him. James did not back down and told daddy where to go:

Daddy: "Now, James, haven't I been good to you? Haven't I given you everything you've ever wanted and more?"

James: "Come on daddy, you know damn well you can't get me with that line. The only thing I've ever received from you is a hard time. I'm going to ask you one more time to leave, and if you don't I'm calling the cops."

Daddy: "I'm going to kill you if you don't let me in. If you're smart, you'll do as I say!"

James pulls out his pistol:

James: "See this gun, daddy? Now don't even think I won't use it on you. Just because mama isn't home doesn't give you the right to come over here and harass me! Also, don't think I won't kill you on the porch and bring drag you inside the house. John told me about you and I know damn well he'd never lie!"

Daddy: "Boy, don't tell me anything about him. I don't want any part of him. In fact, I'm going to do everything in my power to keep him in Mobile."

James (Still holding the pistol): Well, I happen to love John. If you touch him after he gets out, I'll kill you!"

Daddy: "I want to tell you about guns. They're not suppose to be used. I forbid you to use them in this family!"

James (yelling): "I'll use a gun as long as you are screwing up our lives, bastard!"

The police came after James called them.

As 1966 began, things seemed worse. Daddy loved trouble and with age, the more violent he became. Sad thing about it was the police didn't do a damn thing. Daddy had been threatening us for two years. He'd been telling me he was going to kill me and I was very scared for my life. Something had to give. The bottom line was he was going to be a threat as long as he was allowed to roam free.

It was official I'd have to stay in Mobile Detention until Jun. 20 and would be extremely lucky to get out then. Daddy was trying to get an extension for me to stay until at least September. He and the judge met each other halfway. The center was pushing for me to get out March 20 and daddy wanted and extension until Sept. 15, so the judge's final decision in the middle. I knew it would be worth the wait because the judge didn't like daddy either and wanted to see him get nailed too! Years later, I learned daddy wanted to keep me in until March 1967, but the judge got fed up with his nonsense and used the bribe to keep me until June 20 against him. Before it was all over in 1967, he threatened the judge at his sentencing, by saying "You're dead when I get out!"

There was more! Daddy got in trouble again for harassing mama shortly after he attempted to bribe the judge. I hoped daddy would get another violation before the year was out. The police probably wouldn't do a damn thing about it anyway. In reality, if he had anymore violations this year they'd have no choice but to try him and if

found guilty, go to prison for harassment,
endangerment of his family, and bribes. He
finally settled down. It was about time, he'd
given us enough trouble!

March 1966. Gang Leader, Butch Jones is killed.

I feared it would happen and it did. I remember the day like it was yesterday. It was Mar. 16, 1966. That was the day the former leader of the Bad Boys Gang (BBG) was shot in the head and killed by the police. I looked forward to seeing him after I got out of juvenile. This was Butch Jones. He'd robbed a bank, the police caught up with him and he refused to go back to prison, so he holed himself in an abandoned house and started shooting at him. They had no other choice but to shoot him because he'd already said he wouldn't be taken alive. He still had a year left on his parole and he knew he was going back to prison since he was 20, so he pulled out all the stops. It was a sad situation and it made me feel thankful that I at least had one parent who cared. This made me think and I knew I'd never go back to my old ways again.

May 1966. Daddy strikes again.

It was finally here, May 1966. This was a very exciting time for me. I only had six more weeks to go in here, daddy would finally be behind bars, and I would FINALLY get on with my life. By this time, I was positive I would be out on the date discussed earlier because daddy struck again. This time he threatened James with a double barrel shotgun. James shot back at him, nearly hitting him in the head! He nearly scared him half to death, which was good because he left us alone for a good long while. Then, James called the police. He'd threatened because he claimed that James was a good for nothing idiot who didn't deserve to live. It was only a matter of time now.

Daddy's Past (1922-66)

Until now I haven't mentioned anything about daddy's past, at least not prior to 1957. Now that I'm older and understand things better, I know what his problem was and why he's like he was. I don't like him and what he put us through, but I feel sorry for him in almost as many ways. He was born Jerry Allan Cooper on May 23, 1922, in Lincoln, Nebraska. As a boy, he was treated very well. His mother and father gave him everything he needed. In 1929, the family moved to Biloxi, Mississippi. Two years later, on July 31, 1931, his mother died of a stroke at age 37, when he was nine.

His father was not the same after his mother died. His dad blamed him for his wife's death and beat him every time he talked about his mother, not allowing him to grieve. In 1938, at age 16, he ran away from home. He stayed gone until 1945, working odd jobs. In Biloxi, he met my mother Sandy. After two years of dating, they married in 1947. She was six months pregnant with James. At the time, he seemed like he'd overcome his childhood problems and was a very nice man. He always helped people, loved his family and had many friends. I vaguely remember him ever being that way, but I don't believe mom would've married him otherwise.

In 1954, when I was five, he began to change. Before the year was out, he became very abusive, lost many of his friends, disassociated himself with his extended family and lost control of his life. In 1958, his father, my grandfather, died at age 70. This was when he completely lost control and started treating us the same way his dad treated him. By 1962, he was no longer married to mama and declared mentally imbalanced and was charged with child abuse, which brings us to the present. He has had one restraining order violation after another and he would soon go on trial and be sentenced.

June 20, 1966. FREE AT LAST!

The rest of the above goes: "Free at Last, Free at Last, Thank God Almighty I'm free at last!" These were the words of the famous Martin Luther King, Jr. With the exception of my wedding day, this was the happiest day of my life. I couldn't believe I was OUT OF HERE! Shout it from the rooftops, I'M OUT OF HERE! I was finally done with Mobile Alabama Detention Center and I was going home after two years, five months, five days, and four hours. Everyone knew I was glad to be out because I screamed out the car window at people on the freeway all the way home. I had Jan. 15, 1964 to Jun. 20, 1966 behind me. I was ready to get on with my life!

Unfortunately, the celebrations would last a very short time. There was still a quite a bit of unfinished business to take care of. Without the protection of being in juvenile and daddy knowing I was out, there would be other dangers. Many questions went through my mind:

"What if he caught up with me completely off guard while walking down the street to the store?"

"Would he pay me a visit the first night I was home?"

"Would he try to harm any new friends I make to get back at me?"

These and many other questions loomed over my head. Daddy was still out in public and I was scared for my life. However, I didn't hear from him until August. The only thing he did was write me to express how sorry he was that I was out of juvenile. This worried me more because this gave him two extra months to plan something.

"I didn't know….Was he waiting for the perfect time to strike??"

To Be Continued

End of Part III

PART FOUR

High School and the Freedom Years: The Life
of John Cooper from June 1966 to July 1969

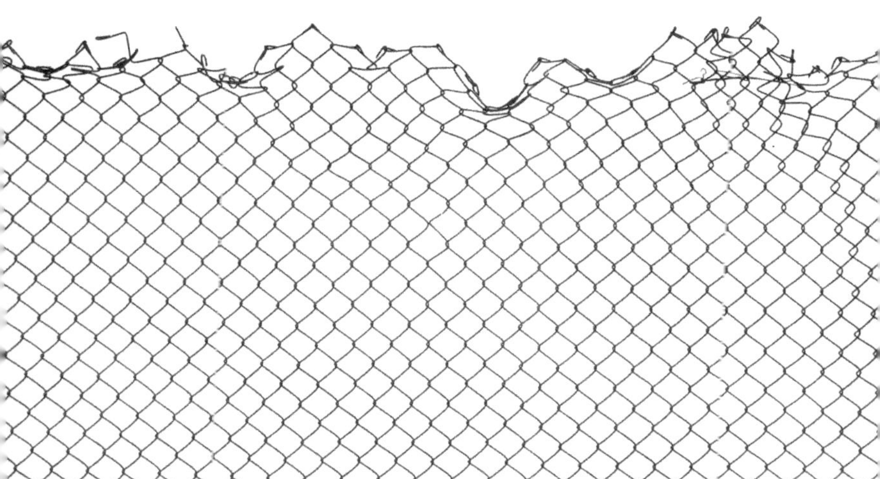

July 1966

I'd been out of "The Pen" a month now and it was wonderful. It was wonderful to be back with my old gang who had gotten straight too. I hadn't seen these guys in two and a half years. Immediately I could see the ones who had changed and the ones who had not. The girls changed for the better as well. Unfortunately, I didn't have one yet, but it didn't take long. Besides, I was with my old gang and I loved it. The only one missing was Butch.

I still had a major problem, however. Given the fact that daddy had treated me so bad in the past, I had a hard time getting along with adults, especially men. It took me a very long time to learn that most male adults were not like daddy. In fact, 99.5% of them were not like that at all, thank God. I simply had to be patient and do what I was told. It wasn't going to be easy, but it didn't take long. Needless to say, the gang was very glad to see me too.

The Meeting

Gang: "Say, Johnny, how's it going?

Me: "Great, thanks for asking. Everything is much different now that I'm no longer in what I like to call 'hell.'"

Mike Jones: "I know that's right."

Me: "Yeah, I heard about Butch."

Mike: "He had so many problems, but we're all good guys now, believe it or not. It's kind of like the movies except this is real. It's really a miracle that we've all changed. We just all made a pact to give back to the community everything that we took away from them in the past. Ironically, we help most of the people that we hurt so much in the past and everyone loves us now."
Me: "I would love to be able to help, but I don't know how much I'll be able to do right now. I'm still having trouble with my old man. He's still threatening us as well as talking and doing his nonsense."

Mike: "I'm sorry to hear that. Hopefully something will happen soon to make life better for you. As you know I don't like your father either. He's a real idiot."

Me: "Tell me about it! All I know is I'll feel better when he's off the streets and behind bars. I guess I better go. I don't like being out past nine. I don't want to give mama, James and Joe any reason to worry."

Mike: "Check you later. Take it easy."

It was very strange to see how much they'd changed, except for Butch. To be honest, I was concerned when I got out if I started hanging out with them; I'd go back to being in trouble again and would have to find new friends. Turns out, I didn't have to do that at all. I mean, before I went in, they were much worse than me. It goes to show what happens when you turn to the Lord and start doing His will. He certainly knew what he was doing and He made a change in their lives too. It was a wonderful reunion and I wouldn't trade them for anyone in the world.

One Month Later, Daddy's Back

Daddy wasn't out of my life yet. He violated the restraining order again. It was for threatening mama and I again. He told me I had no business being in school or at home, but in juvenile. He gave me a choice to either go back to juvenile or he'd kill me. I told him I'd rather die than go back to juvenile; at least I'd be in heaven! I even refrained from calling the police until he started threatening my life and then I had no choice.

Daddy: "Ok now, John, come on with daddy. I will treat you good from now on son."

Me: "Since when?! Daddy, all you know is how to make everyone miserable!"

Daddy: "Ok, I'll put it this way. If you don't come with me I'll kill you, how's that?!"

Me: "I see how you treat James and Joe. I'll be damned if Joe has the kind of life I had. Now, if you don't want me to shoot you right here, I advise you to stay right where you're at until the police come. Trust me I'll kill you!"

(A few minutes later, the police came)

Daddy (Yelling): "Ok son, I'll be back, you watch!"

December 12, 1966, Daddy is Arrested for Attempted Murder

Daddy came back just like he said he would. He almost killed me. I couldn't believe I officially had the power to take him to court! He literally almost killed me! He nearly chopped me up with a hatchet! If it hadn't been for James, I would've been lying in the morgue! However, daddy's murder attempt was not totally unexpected. We knew since September he would try to kill someone, namely me. The reason for our suspicion was in the last days before his conviction; he got to where he loved carrying a hatchet around to threaten people with. He'd also carried guns and knives, threatening people on the streets with them! This is how I knew we'd soon be resting easy. On the night of Dec. 11, it finally happened. It was not the right thing to do. Threatened, hell! He actually tried to kill me! Here's the story.

I was at the side of the house when he grabbed me by the throat and said:

Daddy: "Don't you move, you bastard! I told you that I was going to kill you and you better believe I will."

He continued saying:

Daddy: "I've always hated you. You're going to realize I am your father. I brought you into this world and damn, I'm taking you out!"

About that time James took up for me. With the hatchet in his hand, daddy started to swing at me. As the hatchet came down on my head, James stepped out, punched him and he hit the ground, daddy lost the hatchet. After that, James picked it up off the ground and said:

James: "If I were you, daddy, I wouldn't try to get up. I will kill you if you do. If you ever do kill John, you might as well kill me, mama and Joe. Of course you'll never succeed because any one of us will kill you if the other doesn't succeed."

At that point daddy got up like he was walking away, but that was not his intention. He grabbed the hatchet, walked toward James and said:

Daddy: "Now you bastard, you're right, I'll kill you, John, Mama, and…."

BANG!!

James shot daddy very close to the heart! He almost killed him! I couldn't believe he actually shot him!! To this day, I don't think daddy believed it either!

Daddy: (Slumping to the ground like he'd died): "YOU SHOT ME! I didn't think you had the guts!"

Me: "Damn James! I didn't think you were serious!"

James: "Well John, I told him I would! I didn't want to do it and it wasn't easy, but I had no choice. It was either us or him."

We called the police shortly after and James stayed until they arrived. We told them what happened. Daddy was taken to the hospital for surgery to remove the bullet. Mama saw the whole thing from the front porch, but unfortunately there wasn't anything she could do to stop it. We could now rest easy. Daddy was finally in custody and off the streets, never to harm anyone again. Three weeks later, on Jan. 2, 1967, he was released from the hospital and taken to the county jail. The next thing was to set a hearing. But for the time being, he was not roaming the streets. This freedom still had much left to be desired!

June 16, 1967, Daddy is convicted on all counts.

This was an important day. *This was the day daddy's accusations turned out to be convictions. Daddy had known since February that he would not only be tried for attempted murder, but for the bribes to the judge to keep me in detention. He was madder than hell, but it served him right for what he'd done. The judge didn't like him either. In addition to his conviction of bribery, attempted murder, harassment, and refusal to pay child support were added. This went in my diary, even though I had no intentions of putting it in there. I was very glad daddy was going to prison. This was his final home. He was sentenced to 99 years without parole. He remained there from Oct. 1967, until his death on April 4, 1984. The state awarded us his house. Georgia and I moved there when we married and we lived there until 1984.*

That summer, I had a young lady on my radar. Her name was Georgia Templeman. I was on her radar too. She was always at the drive in theater where me and my buddies would hang out and watch movies. I started talking to her and immediately I knew she was someone special. However, she had a boyfriend. I wasn't too concerned about it because I knew they were on the outs. Besides, it wasn't like I was looking for anything serious. I was still enjoying freedom too much. I knew the odds were in my favor. I was just waiting for the appropriate time.

August 1967, Times Are Changing.

With daddy out of the way and no longer a threat and our family at ease, we welcomed a much needed change. 1967 was one of the best years of my life. First of all, this would be my last visit to the jail to see daddy before he went to prison. He was transferred to San Quentin in California. Secondly, this was my first year in public school, and finally, it was the first year Georgia and I were together. She was important because she shaped me into a more open and gentler person. I'd have to say if it hadn't been for her, I would've probably gone back to my old ways.

Mobile County Jail, the Last Visit

On Aug. 27, I unwillingly went to see daddy for the last time. After all, he nearly killed me and I wanted to tell him to "go to hell" for the last time. Mama declined at the last minute but James and Joe were there. Mama said it was too hard to see him as a criminal after he used to be so different. She still loved him, but it got to the point to where she couldn't be with him. I also felt it was important to see him because he was our father. James was 20, I was 18, and Joe was eight. I thank God constantly that he hasn't gone through what I went through at his age. He was really a cute kid and I loved him. As for daddy, nothing had changed:

Daddy: "Oh Officer, here come my ungrateful sons!"

Me: "Hi daddy, how are you doing?"

Daddy: "I was alright until you ingrates showed up!"

James: "Yep, you haven't changed a bit!"

Daddy: "I'm still going to kill you two."

Me: "You see, you see, that's the reason why you're in here because of stuff like that! You just can't behave, can you?!"
Daddy: "I don't have to act decent anymore. I'm going to prison anyway!"

Me: "Well, I hope you realize this is the last time we will ever get to see you. All I have to say is that your last visit can either be memorable or it can be a living hell."

Daddy: "Well son, I really appreciate you all coming to see me. I know it's too late to apologize, but I'm really sorry for I have put you through."

Me: "Damn daddy, I'm really surprised to hear you say that. That still doesn't change the fact that I don't like you or trust you. I mean, after what you've put me through, how could I?"

Daddy: "Yeah you're right. I realize now that I made a huge mistake. I feel terrible for wanting to kill you all so bad, but I honestly never thought I could go to prison."

Me: "Well, that's where you're headed, like it or not. You brought it on yourself."

Daddy (In tears): "Yeah, I'll certainly understand if you never forgive me. The only thing I want to kill you for now is putting me in prison."

Me: "I didn't put you there, you did it to yourself. If I hadn't pressed charges, you would've done everything you can to put me back in juvenile. Think of it this way; at least now you wont' have to get killed or wind up killing yourself. I think I'm actually doing you a favor."

Daddy: "Yeah. Well John, I wish you the best. I know you assume I go to hell right?"

Me: "Yes daddy, it's possible, but not necessarily. Here's a Bible. It's your choice whether you do right or not. Let me ask you, you've been to church, but do you believe in Jesus?"

Daddy: "No son, I don't. I mean, I didn't, but I do now! Take care now and bring in the others."

Me (In tears): "Sure thing. This is it, daddy. God Bless you."

The Theater, Six Weeks Later

I loved this place. We'd been coming here every since I left detention. It was where one of the best nights of my life took place. Remember that girl I was talking about? Well, I finally had my first chance to be with her and I used it wisely. While my friends and I were watching a movie, I discovered her and her boyfriend fighting and yelling at each other. It looked like it was about to get really ugly, so I went to see what I could do. I did and apparently that was what she was waiting for. The rest was history:

Me: "Hey guys, this movie isn't very good to me how about you all? How do you feel about it?"

Mike Jones: "No, I can't say that I like it either. I'll tell you what's more exciting."

Me: "What's that?"

Mike: "That cute little blonde fighting with that scum boyfriend of hers."

It was then I realized it was Georgia. Did I have a chance with her after all, could this be the night, just as I was about to give up?

Me: "Oh my God, he slapped her!"

I was unable to stand still. Sure I was a little nervous about making a move but at this point it was about defending an innocent girl. I ran over to the guy and started defending her:

Me (Yelling): "Hey, what the hell do you think you're doing? I don't quite allow for you to treat a lady like that in my presence!"

Boyfriend (Pushing): "Yeah well, this isn't any of your damn business, so beat it you rebel punk!"

Me: "Did I ask you if this was any of my business?! I don't give a damn about the argument. Hell, you can argue all you want. However, you don't EVER slap a female! You got that?!"

Boyfriend: "Dude, you're pushing it! I've already told you to beat it or I'll turn you into a piece of meat to cook when this pavement gets hot again tomorrow!"

At that point, the guy tried to hit me; I blocked it and punched him in the stomach. When he tried to get up I kicked him in the head and then he gave up.

Me: "Yeah, you are just so damn tough! I figured you were going to put me on the ground to get cooked in the morning. Oh I know; you just aren't as much of a bad ass as I thought you were! I learned that little move several years ago in juvenile. If you'd like to try something else, be my guest. I'm sure I know several more moves. Also, I don't EVER want to see you go near this girl again! Do you understand?

Boyfriend: (As he fell to the ground): "Yes."

On the way back to the car, Georgia came to thank me. She was even more beautiful up close. When I walked back to the car I was a little shy toward her:

Georgia: "Hey, before you leave, I would like to thank you for handling that guy for me. My intention has been to get rid of him for quite sometime and now I have a great reason. I want to tell you that he never hit me until tonight. This is 1967. I don't think a woman should let her man tell her what to do anymore!"

Me: "Well, I don't know if you're telling the truth about the hitting or not, but it's not relevant. At least it sounds like you have enough common sense to get away from him now."

Georgia: "You're telling me."

By now, we were looking at each other over very well. When our eyes met, I knew we were very much in love:

Georgia: "WOW! What a wonderful feeling!"

Me: "I know."

Georgia: "Can I have your number? I would like to call you sometime. My name is Georgia Templeman."

Me: "Pleased to meet you, Georgia. My name is John Cooper and yeah, I'll call you. My number is 655-2893."

Georgia: "I guess I better give you mine as well, huh? It's 655-4391."

Me: "I'll keep in touch. I can already tell this is the beginning of a beautiful friendship."

Georgia: "How do you know that?"

Me: "Because it just feels right."

Georgia: "Oh yeah, I know what you mean. It's kind-of weird, huh?"

Me: "Bye."

On the way back to the car, all of my friends were hollering at me because they knew I'd scored. I explained to them, if I hadn't interfered, she could've been seriously hurt. I also mentioned if they should ever have an experience like that, they'd know it too. All I knew was I was going to marry Georgia Templeman!

The First Date-Things between Georgia and John Begin to "Heat Up."

Diary: <u>October 17, 1967</u>

Here's the big story. I went out with Georgia for the first time after a couple of months of courting. It was really difficult because I didn't feel like I was ready for a date. However, Georgia kept asking "When are we going out? It's been a month now." I kept saying I didn't know. But finally, after asking the same thing over and over, I was ready to go out. There are two things I'll never forget. First, I was getting my driver's license. Second, the night I officially began my lifelong romance with Georgia Templeman.

On my 18th birthday, I was labeled as "Eighteen and never been kissed." I kissed her on our first date. That was unusual, but I certainly wasn't going to object to her desire. We really enjoyed each other's company that night at the theater. After that, it was so easy to express my feelings and we were perfect together and still are:

Georgia: "Wow Johnny, this is very romantic. I haven't met anyone like you before. Have you ever kissed anyone before?"

Me: "No, can't say that I have."

Georgia (Crawling onto my lap): Well sweetie, let's just say that after tonight, you will no longer be able to say that. The main thing you need to learn is to let a woman take charge of the kiss. I'm going to start kissing you on the lips and I want you to do the same to me, exactly the way I kiss you. When you feel you're more experienced, then you can take control too."

Me: "I'll go for that."

Georgia: "Ok, are you ready? It's not going to be perfect the first time, but you'll get the hang of it. Just kiss me exactly the way I kiss you and you'll learn pretty fast."

Me: "Yes Ma'am, lay one on me!"

About that time she jumped on top of me with her short skirt, pinning me down with her legs. She had me relaxed in no time. She was right, I learned very fast. I still don't remember what movie was playing that night. It was over pretty soon after that. I guess that's what happens when you're in love.

I'd like to share some information about our first date. I picked her up at 8pm and when she came to the door, she looked amazing. She had her thick blonde hair up in a pink bow, wearing a pink v-neck, long sleeved sweater, showing some of her cleavage, wearing a white beaded necklace. She had on a black miniskirt with black pantyhose and black high heeled shoes. She was 17 years old and was filled out. Her measurements were 34D-27-32, and 5'3." I changed my style of dress too. I had long hair, but not after I met Georgia. She didn't like guys with long hair because she thought they looked like fags, so I cut it. I also quit smoking and started dressing more conservative. Sweaters, slacks, and dress shoes now replaced worn out t-shirts, ripped jeans, and worn out shoes. I was a changed man. My friends thought I was crazy. They were right; I was "Crazy in love."

I still had one major problem. I still had trouble getting along with adults, especially males. But, as mentioned, it was all because of daddy. He was gone, but that still didn't change the fact that this was a major problem I had to overcome. The only adult male I could get along with was Georgia's father.

I think it was because he was easy going, soft spoken, and gentle. Georgia and I fought a quite a bit in the early years over this. In fact, it nearly ruined our relationship. For now everything was great. Except for the "Adult Issue," we loved each other to death.

The Engagement
January 1968, Mobile Park

Georgia: "John, why are you looking at me like that?"

Me: "Because I want to ask you a very important question. Besides, you're so dang beautiful and I can't help staring into your beautiful eyes."

Georgia: "Oh yeah? Since when was I so beautiful all of a sudden? Now what do you want to ask me?"

Me (Stalling): "Well; I'll ask you in a little while."

This is what was discussed during our walk in the park. I wanted to pop the question, but I didn't feel the time was right. It was driving her crazy, but I didn't feel comfortable yet. It took three weeks build up my courage. I think she might've had an inkling of what I wanted to ask and she was sure trying to get me to come clean. On Feb. 5, I got the nerve to ask her to marry me. It was at the same place, same time.

Georgia: "John, you're looking at me that way again. Why do you keep looking at me like that?"

Me: "Well honey, I want to ask you something."

Georgia: "Now John, out with it! This has been going on for three weeks now. You've kept me in suspense for too long! Will you ask me already?"

Me (Choking): "Well, I was wondering if you wanted to be my, uh, my. Oh gosh, this is hard for me to say."

Georgia: "Come on, what is it? You might as well tell me."

Me (Sighing): "I was trying to ask you if you wanted to be my, uh, WIFE?! There, I said it!"

Georgia: "Honey, I've been waiting for you to ask me this for awhile now! Of course I do!"

Me: "REALLY?! That's wonderful! Shall I kiss my future bride?"

Georgia: "You certainly may."

After that, Georgia and I found a place at the side of the trail to celebrate our engagement. That was the first time we felt as if we were man and wife. I believe it gave us a chance to role play before we were married. Of course, I can't say what all we did, but that's to be left up to the imagination. However, I can tell you we didn't do anything we'd regret later.

The engagement took place a couple months before my 19th birthday. We didn't know when we were going to break it to our parents. Neither of us was sure they'd approve, but we were determined to ask them anyway. At the time, Georgia was only 17 and she wouldn't be 18 until July 8. There was no way I could support her, but there was always later.

The Breakup

Diary: April 17, 1968- The Second Worst Day of My Life.

The Story

Here's the lowdown. Georgia and I broke up because I got into an argument with the teacher when he got me for talking. Georgia and I were in the same class. I still had problems getting along with adults, especially men. He didn't like it because I argued with him. One thing led to another, it escalated, and we broke up. I felt so stupid! Here's what happened:

Me (Yelling): "Well, I'm sorry I didn't realize I was raising me voice, Mr. George! I really don't like teachers after they scold me, even if it is for talking!"

Mr. George: "Next time you do, you'll find yourself in the office!"

Me (As I was walking out of the classroom): "Who cares? I'll just leave and drop out of school, that way neither one of us will have to worry about it and you can go to hell!"

With that, I slammed the door and stomped down the hall toward the parking lot.

I knew I was in big trouble with Georgia. But, I also felt it was the teacher's fault because he started it. Then again, it was my fault more than it was his because I was talking instead of listening. If I hadn't been trying to impress Georgia, this would've never happened. I waited in the car for her.

It only took a minute before she started chewing me out. I knew she was mad because of the look she gave me prior to me stomping out of class and slamming the door. After all, this was her favorite teacher.

Georgia: "Just because we decided to get married, don't think that we really are!"

Me (Denying my wrong): "What's wrong with you?"
Georgia: "You know good and well what! You know exactly what you did and you know exactly why I'm upset; so don't pretend like you don't know! My ex-boyfriend did that and I will NOT put up with it. If you talk to my teacher like that again, I'll punch you in the mouth!"

Me: "Ok, I know what I did and I'm sorry. You know how many times I've told you about my daddy. I just can't help it when men scold me like that on count of him. I'm trying, but I can't promise you that I'll ever overcome this problem."

Georgia: "This is different. Mr. George is a very nice man and a great teacher. You have no reason to talk to him that way. You've said it yourself a dozen times that you like him and respect him. If you don't overcome this, hate will consume you until you're not fit to deal with. I mean, your daddy is long gone and I understand how there was a need at the time to be that way, but there's absolutely no reason why you should be that way now."

Me: "Look, I don't need a sermon! If I wanted that I'd go to church, so SHUT UP!"

Georgia: "Ok, how about I just get out of your life and let you run it yourself?! It's pretty bad when you don't remember anything as obvious as yelling at the teacher. You'll probably go back to juvenile without me!"

Me: "Do what you have to do! I can't say that I care right now.

Georgia (Walking Away): "Maybe it's best that we split up! You'll apologize, I guarantee you!"

That's my story and I'm sticking to it! Does it sound familiar? That pretty much describes the "Second worst day in my life." It was a very close second to the day I entered juvenile, which, as you know, was the "Worst day in my life." How about you, have you had one? The first few weeks after this happened it was very hard to think about anything else, which proves she was right and I was wrong. It only took a week to realize that, and after three, I was ready to reconcile. How would I go about doing it? I knew I had to admit it, but good grief that was going to be so hard, but I wasn't about to let it go unresolved.

I decided to seek advice from Mr. Templeman. I went to him because I knew he'd give me sound advice. If Georgia and I ever had a problem I could discuss it with him, and boy did we ever have a problem! I figured he knew her much better than I did, so I met him one night at 11. I knew Georgia would be asleep, which gave us the privacy we needed. He's totally the opposite of daddy. He's a very understanding man.

Me: "Hi sir, how are you?"

Mr. Templeman: "Hi John! I've missed you coming around, son. How have you been?"

Me: "I've been better. Honestly, since Georgia and I broke up, it's been hard to function."

Mr. Templeman: "Don't tell anyone this, but she really misses you."

Me: "REALLY?! I'm sure glad to hear you say that. I mean, I kind-of expected it, but to hear someone else say it, makes me feel a lot better! Truth is I know I'm wrong and she's right, but I'm having a very difficult time admitting it to her."

Mr. Templeman: "I know how you feel, believe me. I had the same problem when Mrs. Templeman and I got into an argument, but you have to swallow your pride and admit it. Besides, you have to understand my daughter. She grew up the 'Easier Way' meaning she had a normal childhood. From what I've heard and I don't want to upset you, but you were in juvenile and you didn't grow up the 'Easier Way' like she did. She really isn't used to this."

Me: "I could never get upset with you, sir. You are a very important part of my life and I understand exactly what you're saying. Why do you think I came to you with this problem? I'm having a hard time adjusting as well. I hate to say this, but you're about the only adult male I can talk to without talking back. It's just something I have to practice doing now that my daddy is put away."

Mr. Templeman: "I wouldn't worry about it, son. Just keep working at it and you'll get there. I know how difficult it must've been growing up with a father like that. And another thing, she's not mad at you anymore; she's just making you sweat it."

Me: "I know. Take it easy, and thanks again for the advice."

That's what's unique about Georgia. That was a pretty heated argument but she was able to put it behind her in a day or two. Remember, Georgia and I were in the same class, so we still had to see each other. We weren't speaking yet, but that didn't mean that she wasn't ready to reconcile. She was just waiting for me to let go of my pride. Then it happened, I was able to admit my mistake:

Me: "Georgia, could you come here for a minute, please?"

Georgia (Sarcasm): "What do you want from me, DEAR?"

Me: "I'd like to apologize for what I said to you that day."

Georgia (Holding a grudge): "Oh, you would, HUH?"

Me: "Certainly, yes. I understand what I did and it'll never happen again. I'll work on my problem until it's no more just to spend the rest of my life with you, not to mention to make me a better person."

Georgia: "Well darling, I honestly must say that is a very legitimate and noble thing to say, much less agree to."

Me: "So that's it? Is that all I needed to say?"

Georgia: "That's it. Now you have to do something else before I get mad at you again."

Me: "What's that?"

Georgia: "You don't know!? Kiss me, silly!"

After that, she pulled my head toward her lips and I felt the passion rush back into our bodies.

Me: "Yes Ma'am, I believe we're back together again!"

Georgia: "Well, if not, I don't know what else you'd call it."

Me: "So do you want to go out tomorrow night?"

Georgia: "All right, dear. I'll see you then."

With that out of the way, it was obvious we had to talk about our wedding plans next year. However, we had a major problem. We never told our parents. Since it was rapidly approaching our first anniversary, we figured we'd better bite the bullet and discuss it with them. We both agreed it was time to stop hiding.

Me: "Georgia, I've been doing a lot of thinking lately.

Georgia: (Laughing): "You, thinking? Come on, don't think please. So far nobody's been hurt. Let me do the thinking. I'm going to be running the household soon. We're going to take you men over someday."

Me: "Ha, Ha, very funny. Could you be serious for about two minutes, I have something very important to discuss with you."

Georgia: "What's that?"

Me: "It's about telling our parents about the wedding plans. Don't you think it's about time we tell them what's going on? I don't see any sense in keeping this a secret any longer. I don't think it's fair to them."

Georgia: "Yeah, I've been thinking about that too. When do you want to tell them?"

Me: "I think we should do it as soon as possible. How about we go over to there tomorrow and tell your parents first and then we'll go to Mama's."

Georgia: "Yeah, I think that would be a good idea. My parents will be the harder ones to convince. If we don't get their blessing, there won't be any sense in going to tell your mama. At any rate, we'll still be engaged whether they approve or not."

Me: "The only thing is you're only seventeen and I'm only nineteen. You haven't finished school yet and I'm just now starting college I really think they're going to make us wait. I know the first and second thing their going to ask. First, they're going to ask how we're going to support ourselves, and second they're going to ask about our education. I'm sure not dropping out of school. I want a higher education."

Georgia: "I'm not either, and I also plan to go to college too, married or not. It really doesn't matter. Besides, we don't even plan on getting married for a year.

Me: "Yeah, that's true. Actually that's what we'll tell them. By then, you'll be out of high school too."

December 1968. The Consent

Getting married at a young age is a difficult procedure when you do it right. I would've advised anyone else to at least wait until they're out of school. Before the previous discussion, it took us six weeks to get up the nerve to try for consent, but we finally got it shortly before Christmas.

Mr. Templeman: "John, we understand that you love our daughter very much and I'm sure we'll feel the same way about our younger daughter and son when they find 'The one' too."

Me: "Well sir, I know how difficult it was to give us your approval and I know we're young, but I appreciate it. I must say, though, I was very surprised you'd give us your blessing when we asked. I know I'm still in school and I don't have a way to support her, but I'll get a job very soon."

Mr. Templeman: "Well, I look at it this way. If I'd said no, you all would've probably gone and gotten married anyway. You're both at the age where you'd do the opposite thing anyway, so why not give you my blessing? Besides, there comes a time when you have to let them go and do what they want. They'll either fall or they'll be responsible enough to keep it together. However, we have full faith that you all will survive and I know you'll take care of her."

Me: "Thank you again, sir.

Mr. Templeman: "Don't you think it's about time you called me something other than sir? Dad will do just fine, especially since you never really had a good one."

Me: "Isn't that the truth! Ok dad, I'll see you later."

Mr. Templeman: "Will do."

With Mr. Templeman's blessing, Mama was next. Without it, we wouldn't have gone through with it. Mama was the hardest one to convince, much to our surprise. We didn't get her consent that night. In fact, she wasn't happy about us keeping our engagement a secret. We were concerned the Templeman's would be the hardest to convince because she wasn't out of high school yet, but it took us six weeks to convince Mama. We knew she'd come around, but didn't know when. We almost had to move the wedding back a year from July 1969 because of it. I know much of it had to do with her problems with daddy, but still. In February 1969, we finally got her consent. She was still reluctant but same as the Templeman's, she knew we might be tempted to marry anyway.

Mama: "John dear, I just don't think you all are ready to get married. You aren't even 20 years old yet, not to mention Georgia, who isn't even eighteen yet. Don't you think you should wait until you both are out of college? I mean, what's the big hurry? I'm happy about your decision, she's a great girl, but I'm worried about you not finishing school. Education is very important these days. What will people think?"

Me: "It's not like I'm going to be like daddy if that's what you're concerned about. We both know he had serious emotional and mental issues."

Mama: "I know you'll do okay. It's just hard to picture you being married as a teenager."

Me: "Well mama, it isn't going to be for almost another year. I'll get a job, I turn 20 in March, Georgia graduates the end of May, and she'll turn 18 in July, our wedding date is set for the 26th; and she starts college in September."

Mama: "Okay, I'll give you my blessing. Keep in mind that I'm very reluctant about it, especially since you didn't tell me you were already engaged."

Me: "We're very sorry about that, it's just that we weren't sure how you all would take it and we were trying so hard to work up the nerve to ask. Don't ask me why, we just were."

Mama: "Well, I just figure the same thing the Templeman's. If I don't give you my consent, you'll go off and get married anyway."

Me: "No we wouldn't have. Give us more credit than that. We would've waited as long as we had to. We weren't about to create any issues with you or our future in-laws."

Mama: "Well, I appreciate that. I know you two will make it."

Me: "Thanks so much for your blessing."

Mama: "You all are most certainly welcome."

Six Months later, we were married.

July 26, 1969. The Best Day of My Life

This was it! The day Ms. Georgia Templeman became Mrs. John Cooper. It was a wonderful ceremony and every anniversary since has been like that day all over again. I still don't regret getting married. We were fairly young, but that's the way people did it in those days. It was a wonderful age for the both of us and we have done just fine. This proved that a rebel wasn't necessarily a bad thing. I'd say I've come a long way, from an abusive father to a very happy life. I'd like to close with some final moments from that day.

Mama: "Congratulations son!"

Me: "Thanks mama. You don't know how much we appreciate your approval on this."

Mama: "Oh, don't mention it. Like I said, I know you'll do very well. Now all I have to do is get James and Joe out of the house. You know I'm just joking right? I want them to stay as long as possible."

Me: "You're right about that! Think of it this way, you're not losing a son, you're gaining a daughter in law!"

Mama: "Oh, get over here and take these pictures before I make Georgia a widow!"

We bid everyone farewell, went on our honeymoon and the rest is history! Yeah, don't expect me to give you details on that. I refuse to share!

THE END

EPILOGUE

November 8, 1991

I guess you're wondering what happened right? Well, sorry, all these stories end in a cliffhanger. You're on your own here! I'm just kidding! You know me now and I told you not to worry. As you know, my old buddies from the gang and I went to see a movie at a drive in theater called "The Theatre" in Mobile, Alabama immediately after the last visit with Daddy. I was serious about that being a Cliffhanger, meaning you'll have to conclude for yourself what happens between him and God. You know me by now and you know what kind of man he was and my definition of a "Rebel."

Georgia and I hit it off and eventually married in 1969. Our relationship was fairly rocky. It was very difficult to get her to understand that I was that way because of my problems growing up with an abusive father. However, she drilled it into my head that was no excuse. She was right and I believe this is why children who abuse their children were also abused much in the same way, but fortunately I had that "Rebel Instinct" to do the right thing by having daddy sent to prison. Abuse is a vicious cycle that must be stopped in your generation, otherwise it will continue over and over again. To this day, Georgia is nearly always right when we have discussions. When she says I or the kids stink and need a bath, she's right! I'm just kidding about that, but it's almost like it.

Georgia and I have three beautiful children and live in Montgomery now. We both have great jobs and have had great success. It would be hard to imagine life any other way. It's better to be loved than not loved at all. Daddy never had any love for any of us, and it was difficult, but no one can bring a person down if you don't let them. Mama is always there for us and still is to this day. If it weren't for her, I don't think we'd be having this discussion. Don't take that as nothing but a figure of speech because I didn't let my rough childhood get me down and neither should anyone else.

I HAVE FOUND THE TRUE MEANING OF BEING A REBEL.

THE REBEL

The idea from this book came in 1992. Until that point in my life, I was under the impression that a rebel was a bully and a menace to society until I realized this doesn't have to be. Why not look at a rebel in a positive light?

Is the main character in this story a good or bad influence? I'll let you decide! Hope you enjoy reading it as much as I enjoyed writing it.

I am the author of two books, The Rebel and Touch of Evil. I was born in Irving, TX in 1971, and have lived in the Dallas Area all my life. Im a graduate of Cedar Hill High School in Cedar Hill, TX in 1991, and a graduate of Mountain View College in Dallas in 2000. I currently reside in Cedar Hill, Tx.

BLUEPRINT PRESS
INTERNATIONALE

Locally Love

a relocated christmastime novella

Lori Thorn